D0880956

FAIRY TALE MIX-UPS

Three Blind Mice
Team Up with the
Three Little Pigs

written by Paul Harrison
illustrated by Mariano Epelbaum

capstone

O nce upon a time, there were three little pigs. They all lived happily in their own homes, until the Big Bad Wolf arrived.

The Big Bad Wolf wanted to eat the pigs. He huffed, and he puffed, and he blew down two of the homes!

4

The three pigs decided to move into one home together.

The house was very nice, but it had been built *for* one pig. There just wasn't enough space in the home.

6

To make matters worse, the Big Bad Wolf was still around. He was still hungry for the pigs.

The pigs wanted to leave their small home, but it was too dangerous to leave. The Big Bad Wolf would eat them! What's more, the pigs were running out of food.

On the other side of the forest, three blind mice lived in a farmhouse. The house was lovely and warm. The mice had plenty of food.

But the house was too big for mice who couldn't find their way around.

To make matters worse, the house was owned by Mrs. Farmer. She did not like the three blind mice.

She would chase the mice up, down, and all around to try and chop off their tails.

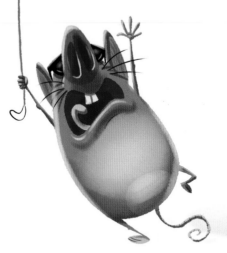

One day Mrs. Farmer chased the mice out of their house. Out in the woods, they bumped into the three pigs. The pigs had **sneaked** out of the house to find food.

The mice and the pigs told each other their sad stories.

"I think I have a plan," said one of the pigs.

As part of the plan, the mice dressed up like the little pigs and went to the pigs' home. Later that day, the wolf climbed down the chimney.

He couldn't believe what he saw!

"Pah!" he said. "The pigs have **shrunk** away to nothing. They would not even be a good snack any more!"

And off he stomped.

As part of the plan, the pigs dressed up
like the mice and went to their farmhouse.

When Mrs. Farmer saw them, she nearly
lost her **bloomers** in shock.

"Mice as big as pigs!" she cried.

And off she ran,
never to return.

So the three blind mice lived in the pigs' home. It was small and **cozy**. They could easily find their way around.

The three little pigs lived in the farmhouse, which had plenty of room.

And they all lived happily ever after.

The Three Little Pigs

The story of *The Three Little Pigs* told by Joseph Jacobs in 1890 is probably the best known version. In Jacobs' story, the three pigs each make a house. One is made of straw, one is made of twigs, and one is made of bricks. The wolf blows down the first two houses but can't blow down the third. He tries to climb down the chimney to catch the pig. He lands in a big cooking pot the pig has put over the fire.

Three Blind Mice

"Three Blind Mice" is a popular children's nursery rhyme from Great Britain. In the rhyme, three blind mice are chased around a house by the farmer's wife. She wants to cut off their tails. The rhyme was first written in 1609, but the one people know today comes from the 1800s.

Glossary

bloomers—big underwear

cozy—warm and comfortable

shrunk—got smaller

sneaked—to creep without being seen

Writing Prompts

Try telling the story from the wolf's point of view. What would the wolf say about what happened?

Write some directions for the three blind mice, telling them how to get through the forest to the three little pigs' house. Remember: they can't see where they are going! Think of the other senses: hearing, touch, smell, and taste.

Imagine Mrs. Farmer told her story to the newspaper. Write the newspaper article.

Read More

Gunderson, Jessica. *No Lie, Pigs (and Their Houses) Can Fly!: The Story of the Three Little Pigs as Told by the Wolf* (The Other Side of the Story). North Mankato, MN: Picture Window Books, 2016

Hoena, Blake. *Three Blind Mice* (Tangled Tunes). North Mankato, MN: Cantata Learning, 2016

Rosen Schwartz, Corey. *The Three Ninja Pigs*. New York: G.P. Putnam's Sons, 2012

The Three Little Pigs. New York: Parragon Books, 2012

Internet Sites

Facthound offers a safe, fun way to find web sites related to this book. All the sites on Facthound have been researched by our staff.

Here's all you do:
Visit **www.facthound.com**
Type in this code: 9781410983015

Read all the books in the series:

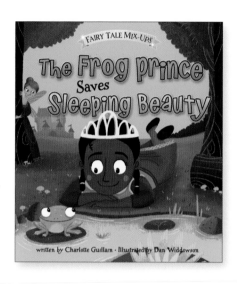

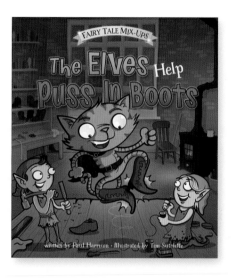

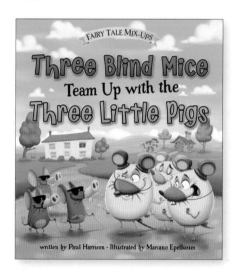

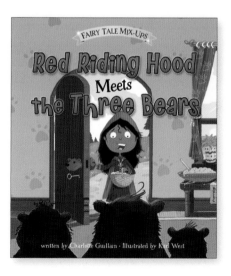

Visit www.mycapstone.com

23

Edited by Penny West
Designed by Steve Mead
Original illustrations © Capstone Global Library Ltd 2016
Illustrated by Mariano Epelbaum, Astound US
Production by Steve Walker
Originated by Capstone Global Library Limited
Printed and bound in [select]

20 19 18 17 16
10 9 8 7 6 5 4 3 2 1

Library of Congress Cataloging-in-Publication data is available on the Library of Congress website.

ISBN: 978-1-4109-8301-5 (library binding)
ISBN: 978-1-4109-8309-1 (paperback)
ISBN: 978-1-4109-8313-8 (eBook PDF)

Summary: The Big Bad Wolf keeps trying to eat the three little pigs. The farmer's wife keeps chasing the three blind mice. If they work together, maybe they can solve each other's problems.

Printed and bound in China

PO007731LEOF16